# Robyn's Art Attack

Hazel Hutchins

# Robyn's Art Attack

Illustrations by Yvonne Cathcart

**First Novels**

Formac Publishing Company Limited
Halifax, Nova Scotia

The development and pre-publication work on this project was
funded in part by the Canada/Nova Scotia Cooperation
Agreement on Cultural Development. Formac Publishing
Company Limited acknowledges the support of the Cultural
Affairs Section, Nova Scotia Department of Tourism and
Culture. We acknowledge the financial support of the
Government of Canada through the Book Publishing Industry
Development Program (BPIDP) for our publishing activities.

We acknowledge the support of the Canada Council for the Arts
for our publishing program.

**National Library of Canada Cataloguing in Publication Data**

Hutchins, H. J. (Hazel J.)
    Robyn's art attack / Hazel Hutchins; illustrations by
    Yvonne Cathcart.

(First novels; #23)
ISBN 0-88780-565-5 (bound) — ISBN 0-88780-564-7 (pbk.)

    I. Cathcart, Yvonne  II. Title.  III. Series.

PS8565.U826R6188 2002      jC813'.54      C2002-901180-9
PZ7.H96162Ro 2002

Formac Publishing
Company Limited
5502 Atlantic Street
Halifax, Nova Scotia B3H 1G4
www.formac.ca

Printed and bound in Canada

Distributed in the United States by:
Orca Book Publishers
P.O. Box 468 Custer, WA
USA 98240-0468

Distributed in the UK by:
Roundabout Books (a division of
Roundhouse Publishing Ltd.)
31 Oakdale Glen, Harrogate,
N Yorkshire HG1 2JY

Table of Contents

# 1
## Robyn's Pick

My name is Robyn and I eat lions for breakfast.

Tigers for lunch.

Bears for supper.

That's the way you have to be when you decide to go against the entire class at school.

"Congratulations, Robyn," said Ms. Wynn on Friday afternoon. "It looks like you get to choose where we go for our next field trip."

Three times a year Ms. Wynn stages her "Wild and Wonderful Improvement

Tests." They're different from most tests. It's not the highest score that gets the attention, it's the most improved score in math, spelling and reading.

Sometimes a kid at the top of the class wins. Sometimes a kid at the bottom of the class wins. This time someone in the middle of the class won. Me!

All eyes turned to me. I should have been happy. I should have been proud. Instead I felt a little trickle of fear run down my back.

There were two official rules.

Rule number one — no trips to Disneyland. Choose somewhere we could reach by walking or by bus.

Rule number two — no action movies. Our field trip had to have at least some educational value.

There was one unofficial rule. As far as our class was concerned, it was the most important rule of all.

Most important rule of all number three — choose someplace everyone wants to go.

"Pioneer Park," whispered my best friend Marie.

"Science centre," whispered Ari from across the aisle.

"Hockey rink!" called Grant from the back of the class.

Grant always calls out hockey rink. He says maybe we could tour the ice-making plant and drive the machine

that cleans the ice —
educational and fun.

Other places kids like are
the zoo, the planetarium and
the chocolate factory. I wasn't
going to choose any of them.

I squared my shoulders. I
took a deep breath.

"I choose the art gallery,"
I said.

I was expecting groans. I
was expecting moans. I was
expecting Grant to make
barfing sounds.

Instead there was silence.
And more silence. And more
silence.

Finally, from the back of
the class, Grant spoke up very
clearly and politely.

"Great idea, Robyn," he
said. "And after that we can

go to the library and do something even more interesting like look at books and sit around quietly."

This was going to be even worse than I expected.

# 2
# A Budding Artist

"I don't get it Robyn, are you trying to get everyone mad at you?"

That's what my best friend, Marie, asked me on our way home after school. She didn't wait for an answer. She just kept talking.

"Nobody, NOBODY wants to go and hang around the art gallery. A field trip is supposed to be fun. Kids are supposed to be able to talk and visit and maybe run around a bit instead of sitting in class all day."

"I need to go to the art gallery," I said.

"Why?" asked Marie.

"It's a secret," I said.

"What kind of secret?" asked Marie.

I didn't want to tell anyone, at least not yet. Marie, however, wasn't about to leave me alone.

"I don't tell secrets," said Marie. "You know that. What is it?"

"I'm going to be an artist when I grow up," I said.

Marie got all blotchy in the face.

"What's wrong?" I asked her.

"I don't want to say it. If I say it you'll be mad at me," said Marie.

"Say it," I told her. "I won't be mad at you."

"Last month you were going to be a singer. And before that you were going to be someone who studies bears. And before that you were going to be a tightrope walker."

Sometimes I wish my best friend Marie wasn't quite so good at remembering things.

"This time is different," I said. "This time I've already started. One of my pictures is going to be in the newspaper."

"In *The Daily News*?" asked Marie.

I nodded.

"Remember when Ms. Wynn's friend came to talk to us about being a journalist?

He said he was starting a kids' page with the comics on the weekend and we could send our art to it. I sent some."

"And they chose your art?" asked Marie.

This next bit was a little tricky.

"They can't tell you ahead of time. You have to wait for the paper to come out. But I got a letter that says it without actually saying it."

Marie looked like she didn't believe me.

"It won't be the first time people have liked my art," I said. "A couple of years ago I won the Spring Flowers Colouring Contest at the grocery store."

Marie looked around. The three Gs — Grant Smith, Ari Grady and Linden Abergeiser — were walking on the other side of the street.

"Hang on a minute," said Marie.

The Three Gs are the most annoying boys in the class when they're together, but Ari on his own is OK. Marie came back with Ari.

"I don't get it, Robyn," said Ari. "Are you trying to get everyone mad at you?"

"Don't even ask her about it," said Marie. "Just tell her about the Spring Flowers Colouring Contest."

"You mean the one where they can't decide so they put all the entries in a box and just draw one out?" asked Ari.

"They don't do that," I said. "It's a contest. They choose the best one."

"Nope," said Ari. "My mom works there. They can never decide so they just draw one out of the box."

"That doesn't mean anything," I said to Marie. "Wait and see. On Sunday."

# 3
# The Phone Call

*Thank you for sending your pictures to* The Daily News Kids' Page. *Be sure to read the paper on Sunday to see the name and work of the special artist chosen!*

When I got home I read my letter. Of course my art had been chosen. The word "sure" was in red ink. The word "special" was underlined. Why would they even send me a letter like that if my art hadn't been chosen?

I got out paper and

coloured pencils. I drew a picture of a bear. It turned into a dog with funny ears. I gave it a hat to cover its ears. I gave it a bow tie and a vest. It looked like a rich and famous dog on the way to somewhere important. I was a good artist!

All Saturday I drew pictures. So long as I was drawing I felt sure that the letter meant I was going to win.

On Sunday I ran to the apartment next door to borrow the paper from Mr. and Mrs. Kelly. The Kellys have ten-month-old twins named Abigail and Angela. I played with the twins while Mr. and Mrs. Kelly finished reading the paper. It seemed to take longer than usual.

Finally I took the paper back to my own apartment. I gave my mom the news part. I took the colour comics and kids' page into my bedroom. I closed the door. I opened the paper.

My art was nowhere to be found.

Someone else's art was there instead.

There must have been a mistake!

I phoned the newspaper. I asked for the person who had visited our school. I remembered his name because it had lots of the letter "G" again — Gary Gillis. I also remembered to be very polite.

"I was wondering if some of

the art is held over for other weeks?" I asked.

"Nope," said Mr. Gillis. "We choose from a new batch each week."

"I was wondering if there were two artists chosen this week and one of them just got missed. It's because of the letter I got. It didn't actually say I won, but it sounded like it."

"Everyone gets the same letter," said Mr. Gillis. "It's just meant to be polite."

As politely as I could I said good-bye and hung up the phone.

Now I was really mixed up.

And I'd made everyone in the class mad at me for nothing.

# 4
## Art Gallery or Bust

On Monday morning Marie was waiting at the end of my block.

"Hi, Robyn!" she said cheerily. "Have you decided where we'll go for the field trip? Can we go to Pioneer Park?"

"Why do you think I've changed my mind?" I asked her.

"Because your art wasn't in the paper. I looked. If your art wasn't in the paper, you're not going to want to go to the art gallery. I know you."

Marie hadn't said, "I told you so." She wasn't acting mean either. Suddenly, however, part of me was very annoyed with Marie.

Just then Ari came around the corner.

"Hey, Robyn — did you make up your mind? Are we going to the science centre?"

I looked at Marie. I looked at Ari.

"You told him!" I said. "You told him the secret!"

"No I didn't," said Marie. "I just told him you were going to change your mind. A zillion kids from our class phoned me because they were mad at you. I got tired of it. I told them it was just a mistake and you'd change your mind.

I didn't tell them why."

"What's the secret?" asked
Ari. "Why did you change
your mind?"

Grant Smith came trotting
up the street.

"Hockey riiiiiiink!" he
called.

"We're going to the art
gallery!" I said.

I crossed the street and
walked to school on my own.

# 5
## A Good Idea

"Stay little," I told the twins that day when I went over to play with them after school. "Don't grow up. When you grow up everyone, even your very best friend, starts telling you what's going on in your head and then they tell you what to do. And the more people tell you what to do, the more you won't want to do it."

"What don't you want to do?" asked Mrs. Kelly.

I told Mrs. Kelly about the class field trip. I didn't tell

her why I'd chosen the art gallery. There was something really bugging me about the newspaper and my drawing and the letter. I was still trying to figure it out. But I told her the rest of it.

"It will depend on what the art gallery is like," said Mrs. Kelly. "Do you mean the big one downtown?"

I nodded.

"We could visit it ahead of time to check it out," said Mrs. Kelly. "I used to go to galleries back home but I've never seen this one. We could go after school tomorrow. You could bring Marie."

"What about the twins?" I asked.

"We can roll them around

in the stroller. They'll probably fall asleep."

I looked at Abigail and Angela. They were a lot more active than they used to be. They were crawling and climbing and pulling themselves up to try and stand.

The phone was ringing when I went home for supper. It was Marie.

"Are you still mad at me?" she asked.

"Yup," I said.

"Even if I'm sorry?" asked Marie.

"Well, maybe not quite as mad," I said. "Besides, I know how you can make it up to me."

If we were taking the twins

to the art gallery, we'd need all the help we could get.

# 6
## The Twins Go Nuts!

"Look out! Abby's headed for the stairs!"

"Quick! Head off Angie! She's crawling under the rope!"

"They've got a whole room of abstract art! A whole room of Impressionists! A whole gallery of the Group of Seven and Canadiana! And some of these contemporary exhibits look really wild!"

It started almost the minute we were in the door. The twins came alive. So did Mrs. Kelly.

I chased the twins. Mrs.

DO NOT TOUCH
Thank you

Kelly chased the art. Marie was supposed to help me chase the twins but she isn't used to little kids the way I am, and besides, with Mrs. Kelly going, "Look! Look at this one!" she kept getting distracted.

I was distracted too. Way too distracted. The twins scrambled out of the stroller, squirmed in my arms and tried to touch everything with "Do Not Touch" on it.

Finally I told Mrs. Kelly I'd take the twins back to the lobby where they could touch things that didn't matter — like the water fountain and the benches. I didn't even bother telling Marie. She was off staring at some picture that looked like triangles gone wild.

In the lobby the twins were a whole lot better. They sat in the stroller and looked up at the fan overhead going around and around and around. I stared at a great big painting on the wall.

The painting was of a city street. At least, from a distance it was a city street. Up close it was something else. Up close it was made of a million teeny-tiny advertising slogans in all sorts of colours and forms. The way it was two things at once was making something important click at the back of my brain.

I would have stared at that picture a whole lot longer

except the twins were sick of looking at the fan and were scrambling out of the stroller again.

Ahhhhhhhh!

# 7
# The Letter

That night, when we got back from the art gallery, I was exhausted.

I'd also figured something out.

I wrote a letter.

*Dear Mr. Gillis,*
*You said on the phone that the same letter goes to everyone who enters your kids' art-page contest and it's only meant to be polite.*
*I think the letter is like the picture in the lobby of the art gallery. From a distance it*

*looks like an ordinary city street. That's the polite part. Up close it's made up of all sorts of advertising slogans. That's the sneaky part.*

*The sneaky part of your letter is that you want kids to think they might have won so they will be sure to keep checking the kids' page and their parents will keep buying your paper.*

*Sincerely,*
*Robyn*

I asked my mom for a stamp. I went to the box at the corner and mailed the letter. As soon as it had gone down the chute, part of me felt better.

And part of me felt worse.

Why is life like that? One moment you think you've got a problem all figured out and you do something about it. The next moment you realize maybe you didn't think about things quite enough in the first place.

Gary Gillis had come to our class because he was a friend of our teacher. He'd done it to be nice, as a favour.

What if Mr. Gillis read my letter and felt really bad? What if he got really mad about me writing it? What if he told Ms. Wynn? Why hadn't I thought about that part before I wrote the thing?

# 8
## Nervous Nellie

I knew I was safe for a day or two. Letters take a day or two to get where they are going. By Friday, however, I was getting really, really nervous. When Ms. Wynn called me to the front of the room "to talk with her about something" I figured I was done for.

"Maybe I shouldn't have written it," I told Ms. Wynn. "I know that Mr. Gillis did us a favour when he came to talk to our class. But I didn't write it to be nasty. I only wrote it because it's the truth."

"What are you talking about, Robyn?" asked Ms. Wynn.

"You mean you haven't heard from Mr. Gillis?" I asked.

"I saw him last night," said Ms. Wynn. "He did mention a letter, but all he said was that it was interesting."

"Then you didn't call me up here because you're mad at me?" I asked.

"I called you up because I'm going to send a letter home to parents today," said Ms. Wynn. "I want to check that we're still going to the art gallery."

"Actually," I said, and as I said it my mind was turning over about a hundred times a minute. I'd been mad at Marie for figuring out the truth, but she was right. Since my picture wasn't in the paper I didn't care about going to the art gallery. Besides, I'd already been there. "Actually, it doesn't matter any more. I'll go where the class wants to go."

A cheer went up. I was popular again. OK — I wasn't popular — I was just me. But that was OK.

"Wait!"

All eyes turned to Marie.

# 9
## Marie Makes a Sale

Marie had jumped out of her desk and was waving her arms around.

"What is it, Marie?" asked Ms. Wynn.

"The art gallery is way better than I thought it would be. There are huge paintings, gigantic paintings. Some of them are by famous people. Some of them are by people I've never heard of but their pictures are super anyway. We should still go there."

"Marie!" groaned Grant.

"You'll like it, Grant," said

Marie. "There are hockey paintings. You know that picture of the goalie in the white mask? The one that hangs at the skating rink? It's on loan at the gallery. It's even bigger and better in real life."

"Are you sure?" asked Grant.

"I saw it. There are other paintings by the same artist too. I saw all sorts of neat pictures. I even saw a couple of paintings by Picasso," said Marie. "I thought you had to go to some fancy place like Paris to see something by Picasso."

"I thought so too," said Ms. Wynn.

"They've got a design shop

at the back for kids to try different art techniques. And there's a really weird exhibit in the contemporary section that Ari would like, a robotic chair that falls apart and then puts itself back together."

"There is?" asked Ari.

"And there's an ice-cream parlour in the basement with thirty-seven flavours!"

My friend Marie really knows how to sell an idea when she puts her mind to it.

# 10
# A Big Surprise

We went to the art gallery. It was pretty good as a field trip, maybe not a 10 but a 7 or 8 at least.

Grant spent the entire time staring into the goalie mask of Ken Danby's *At the Crease* painting. Ari watched the robotic chair disassemble and assemble itself twenty-three times. I really liked Emily Carr's tall, tall trees. They reminded me of my summers at Thunder Mountain.

I told Mrs. Kelly about our trip when I went over on

Sunday to play with the twins and borrow the paper. She was pleased. She suggested we go again when a new exhibit comes to town. I looked at the twins trying to climb the furniture and told her I'd think about it.

Back in our apartment I gave my mom the news sections. I took the colour comics and kids' page to my bedroom. I was just opening it up when the phone rang. It was Marie.

"You made it! You made the kids' page!"

There was my letter in print. Beside it in another box was a copy of the letter they sent to all the entries to the kids' page. Beneath both was a headline in big red letters.

## YOU TELL US

**Is Robyn right? Is our letter misleading?**

**Yes _____ No _____**

**Send us your vote!**

**And send us any other problem questions...we'll use them in future weeks.**

**Be sure to read the kids' page next week to see your vote.**

Right away my mind began to work overtime. I could think of lots of problem

questions that kids could vote on. Hey, maybe this could be the start of a whole new career — Robyn the investigative reporter!

Be sure to check this spot in the near future for breaking news.

# Two more new novels in the *First Novels Series:*

## Morgan's Birthday

*Ted Staunton*
*Illustrated by Bill Slavin*
Nothing can spoil Morgan's birthday —
except maybe Aldeen Hummel, the Godzilla
of Grade Three. When Morgan's mom makes
him invite Aldeen to his party, he expects the
worst. But a really cool present saves the day.

## Lilly's Clever Puppy

*Brenda Bellingham*
*Illustrated by Elizabeth Owen*
Lilly gives her brother Mac a robot puppy,
Bitsy, for his birthday. The other children tell
him it's not a "real" dog. But when a friend's
beagle gets stuck on thin ice, Bitsy shows
what a robot puppy can do.

# Look for these *First Novels*!

**Meet Duff**
Duff's Monkey Business
Duff the Giant Killer

**Meet Jan**
Jan's Awesome Party
Jan on the Trail
Jan and Patch
Jan's Big Bang

**Meet Lilly**
Lilly's Good Deed
Lilly to the Rescue

**Meet Robyn**
Robyn's Best Idea
Robyn Looks for Bears
Robyn's Want Ad
Shoot for the Moon, Robyn

**Meet Morgan**
Morgan's Secret
Morgan and the Money
Morgan Makes Magic
Great Play, Morgan

**Meet Carrie**
Carrie's Crowd
Go For It, Carrie
Carrie's Camping Adventure

**Meet Arthur**
Arthur Throws a Tantrum
Arthur's Dad
Arthur's Problem Puppy

**Meet Fred**
Fred and the Flood
Fred and the Stinky Cheese
Fred's Dream Cat

**Meet Leo**
Leo and Julio

**Meet the Loonies**
Loonie Summer
The Loonies Arrive

**Meet Maddie**
Maddie Tries To Be Good
Maddie in Trouble
Maddie in Hospital
Maddie Goes to Paris
Maddie in Danger
Maddie in Goal
Maddie Wants Music
That's Enough Maddie!

**Meet Marilou**
Marilou on Stage

**Meet Max**
Max the Superhero

## Meet Mikey
Mikey Mite's Best Present
Good for You, Mikey Mite!
Mikey Mite Goes to School
Mikey Mite's Big Problem

## Meet Mooch
Missing Mooch
Mooch Forever
Hang On, Mooch!
Mooch Gets Jealous
Mooch and Me

## Meet Raphael
Video Rivals

## Meet the Swank Twins
The Swank Prank
Swank Talk

## Meet Will
Will and His World

**Formac Publishing Company Limited**
5502 Atlantic Street, Halifax, Nova Scotia B3H 1G4
Orders: 1-800-565-1975 Fax: (902) 425-0166
www.formac.ca